NODDY IN TOYLAND

Noddy and the Noisy Drum

Collins

An Imprint of HarperCollinsPublishers

NODDY

CLOCKWORK MOUSE

BIG-EARS

MARTHA

TESSIE BEAR

GOBBO

MR PLOD

MASTER TUBBY BEAR

ONKEY

SLY

MR WOBBLY MAN

BUMPY DOG

It was a sleepy morning in Toyland . . .

Noddy was enjoying a nice lie-in when he was woken by the most terrible din.

"What's that?" he cried, leaping out of bed and hurrying across to the window.

It sounded like someone banging on a drum and it was coming from Mr Tubby Bear's house.

"Master Tubby Bear!" Noddy exclaimed.

"Oh, of course, it's his birthday!" Noddy said, guessing that the drum must be Master Tubby's birthday present.

Noddy hoped the terrible noise would stop, but it became even louder because Master Tubby marched right up to his front door.

He knocked fiercely on the door with his drumsticks, grinning mischievously.

"Oh hello, Master Tubby. Happy Birthday!" said Noddy. He tried not to be too cross with him. After all, it was his birthday!

"Thanks for the card, Noddy!" said Master Tubby, beaming.

"You can take me into town to see Martha Monkey," he then announced. "My mother will give you lots of sixpences!"

"Here's an extra two sixpences, Noddy, for being kind to Master Tubby," Mrs Tubby Bear told him just before he set off.

Then she turned to Master Tubby with a wag of her finger. "Master Tubby – no drumming when driving," she said firmly.

"Oh, I promise!" said Master Tubby.

However, it was not long before Master Tubby broke his promise.

"Milko!" he chuckled to himself quietly, lifting his drumsticks. "I'll wake him up!"

Milko was so startled by the sudden din that he dropped all his eggs.

SMASH! SPLAT!

"Look what you've done, Master Tubby! And you promised!" Noddy cried crossly, stopping his car.

Noddy went to say sorry to Milko. He made Master Tubby say sorry to him as well. However, Master Tubby did not really look that sorry!

They had only driven a short way when Master Tubby raised his drumsticks high into the air and –
BANG! WALLOP! BANG!

Noddy was even more cross with Master Tubby than before. He stopped the car.

"Master Tubby!" he shouted. "You're not to drum when I'm driving!"

Master Tubby did not like being told off and so he
climbed sulkily out of Noddy's car.

"I'll find Martha Monkey on my own," he sniffed.
"And I'll play my drum whenever I want. So there!"

Master Tubby eventually found Martha Monkey. She was at the café and she bought him a large ice-cream sundae for his birthday. Master Tubby's eyes were huge as he looked at it.

"Thanks, Martha," he said greedily, licking his lips.

"You can have your ice-cream if you let me borrow your drum!" said Martha Monkey.

Master Tubby was so keen to start on his ice-cream that he gave her the drum straightaway.

"Thanks!" said Martha Monkey as she looped the drum around her own neck. Master Tubby barely heard her, though. He was too busy lapping up his ice-cream!

Martha Monkey left Master Tubby to finish his ice-cream while she marched around with the drum, a happy smile on her face.

"How do you like my drumming, Clockwork Clown!" she asked as she marched this way and that.

The two goblins, Sly and Gobbo, were secretly watching Martha Monkey marching around with her drum.

"Do you want to hear a great idea, Sly?" Gobbo tittered wickedly. "I could cast a Can't Stop Spell on Martha Monkey. The toys will be really cross if she never stops drumming ever again!"

Gobbo began to cast a wicked spell on Martha, hurling
a stream of magic stars at her.

"Now she won't ever be able to stop drumming again!"
he chuckled.

As the spell took effect, Martha Monkey drummed louder and faster. She marched backwards and forwards, left and right.

"Martha! Stop it!" everyone cried as they tried to dodge out of her way. "Don't do that! It's horrid!"

"I can't help it! I can't stop!" Martha Monkey shrieked as her hands kept drumming all on their own. "I wish I could stop but I can't!"

Master Tubby began to cry. "I want my drum Martha Monkey!" he wailed. "It's mine! Come back!"

Martha Monkey kept drumming and marching. Nothing could stop her!

Martha Monkey marched into the countryside next, her hands going up and down all the time with the drumsticks.

"Oh, please help me someone!" she cried. "My arms are getting so tired. I don't want to drum ever again!"

"Oh no!" Noddy exclaimed as Martha Monkey approached Big-Ears' house. "Not that noise again!"

Noddy had gone to Big-Ears' house to have a nice quiet time – well away from Master Tubby's drum!

But when Noddy saw Martha Monkey with the drum he wondered *what* was going on!

As Big-Ears watched Martha Monkey march round and round, drumming for all she was worth, he realised that she could not help it. He invited her indoors where he put a folded table cloth on top of the drum.

"This won't stop you drumming, Martha, but at least it will stop you making any noise!" Big-Ears told her.

"Thank you, Big-Ears!" said Martha, looking a little happier. "But why can't I stop drumming?"

"I believe you may have been put under some nasty spell," he told her, "by Sly and Gobbo!"

Without further ado, Big-Ears, Noddy and Martha
Monkey all went to the goblins' tree.

"I've brought someone to see you!" said Big-Ears
sternly.

And at that Noddy whipped the folded table cloth
away from Martha's drum, so her frantic drumming
started making a horrible noise again.

"Oh no! That's horrid! Oh stop!" shrieked Sly and Gobbo as Martha marched right up to them.

"Gobbo, I'm getting one of my headaches!" cried Sly. "Get rid of that stupid Can't Stop Spell!"

Gobbo quickly hurled another stream of stars towards
Martha. The very next moment, her legs stopped
marching and her hands stopped moving up and down.
"Oh thank you, Big-Ears!" said Martha Monkey.

The awful drumming noise had suddenly stopped and all was peace and quiet again!

Noddy immediately took the drum back to Master Tubby, who had now learnt his lesson. He promised to think of others next time he played his drum.

"Then a very happy birthday to you!" Noddy said as he munched a slice of Master Tubby's cake.

"And a nice quiet one too!" he added with a chuckle.

This edition first published in Great Britain by HarperCollins Publishers Ltd in 2000

3 5 7 9 10 8 6 4 2

Copyright © 1999 Enid Blyton Ltd. Enid Blyton's signature mark and the words
"NODDY" and "TOYLAND" are Registered Trade Marks of Enid Blyton Ltd.
For further information on Enid Blyton please contact www.blyton.com

ISBN: 0 00 136177 5

Reproduction by Graphic Studio S.r.l. Verona
Printed in Italy by Garzanti Verga S.r.l.

MORE NODDY BOOKS FOR YOU TO ENJOY

Noddy and the Artists

Noddy and the Bouncing Ball

Noddy and the Goblins

Noddy Tidies Toyland

Noddy and the Singing Bush

Noddy and the Treasure Map

Noddy is Caught in a Storm

Noddy and the Driving Lesson

Noddy is Far Too Busy

Noddy and the Magic Watch

Noddy the Nurse

Noddy Tells a Story